Kipchak Johnson wrote
this book. He sometimes
looks after sick animals at
his home in Shropshire.
Lots of wild animals live
in his garden - mostly
slugs and snails.

Cassell Publishers Limited
Villiers House, 41/47 Strand
London WC2N 5JE

First published 1991

ISBN 0-304-32517-1

Printed and bound in Hong Kong by Wing King Tong Co. Ltd

THE LIMPING CAT

It was the first day of the summer holidays...

Kitty was worried. She'd lost her cat.
"I hope it's safe!" she muttered.

"Cheer up!" said the others.
"Today's the big day!"

CHEER UP!

Peachy's Mum had promised they
could play in the old shed. But
they had to clean it up first.

"My cat's been missing for three weeks now. And she was pregnant," said Kitty.

"But I'm glad Roger's still here," she said, stroking Wilson's cat.

Peachy looked sad for a moment. "It's a pity Granny's not alive," she said. "She would have known what to do. She was a vet. She used this shed as a store room."

"What shall WE use it for?" asked Wilson.

"Let's make a science lab!" said Peachy.

"No," said Wilson. "Let's make a model railway!"

"I think we should start an old people's home!" said Kitty.

"I want a smugglers' cave!" shouted Bottle.

"Anyway," said Peachy, "let's get started."

"Wow! Roger wants to get in too.
He's been acting very oddly lately!" said Wilson.

"Phew! It's dusty!" said Kitty.
"What's wrong with Roger?" muttered
Bottle. "He keeps getting under our feet!"

"Look! Lots of stuff for the science lab!" said Peachy eagerly.

"Naah!" said the others. "We don't want a science lab."

"Look! Lots of tracks for the railway!" said Wilson.

"Naah!" said the others. "We don't want a railway."

"Look! A bicycle for carrying the old people!" said Kitty, thrilled.

"Naah!" said the others. "We don't want an old people's home."

"Look! Lots of bandages for pirate headbands!" shouted Bottle.

"Naah!" said the others. "We don't want a smuggler's cave."

Roger was hurt.

"Look! He's bleeding!" said Wilson.

"We can use the bandages on Roger's paw,"
said Kitty.

Suddenly another cat miaowed!
Roger leapt to the ladder.

"You can't play up there Roger!
You're injured," said Peachy.
"Come on!" said Bottle. "Let's
look up here."

But Roger was determined to get
up the ladder.
"He's gone mad!" squeaked Bottle.
Even though he was limping, Roger
got there first.

"Roger! Get out of the way!" said Bottle.
"What are you trying to hide?"

"Roger must be the father. He's been trying to find his family!" said Kitty. "Let's make them comfy with these old blankets," said Wilson. "They'll have to stay here for a few weeks yet."

A sudden thought struck them all at the same time. "Why don't we use the shed as an..."

And so they did!